GEO

ALLEN COUNTY PUBLIC LIBRARY

ACPL ITEM
DISCARDED

2/04

Lexile: 210 L

AR/BL: _____

AR Points: _____

D0042201

Buried Treasure

ALL ABOUT USING A MAP

Written by Kirsten Hall

Illustrated by Bev Luedecke

children's press®

A Division of Scholastic Inc.

New York Toronto London Auckland Sydney
Mexico City New Delhi Hong Kong
Danbury, Connecticut

About the Author

Kirsten Hall, formerly an early-childhood teacher, is a children's book editor in New York City. She has been writing books for children since she was thirteen years old and now has over sixty titles in print.

About the Illustrator

Bev Luedecke enjoys life and nature in Colorado. Her sparkling personality and artistic flair are reflected in her creation of Beastieville, a world filled with lovable Beasties sure to delight children of all ages.

Library of Congress Cataloging-in-Publication Data

Hall, Kirsten.
Buried treasure : all about using a map / written by Kirsten Hall ; illustrated by Bev Luedecke.
p. cm.
Summary: Flippet finds a map that appears to lead to buried treasure, but her friends discover a treasure that is "berried" instead.
ISBN 0-516-22894-3 (lib. bdg.) 0-516-24652-6 (pbk.)
[1. Buried treasure–Fiction. 2. Maps–Fiction. 3. Berries–Fiction. 4. Stories in rhyme.] I. Luedecke, Bev, ill. II. Title.
PZ8.3.H146Bv 2003
[E]–dc21
2003001588

Text © 2003 Nancy Hall, Inc. Illustrations © 2003 Bev Luedecke. All rights reserved. Published by Children's Press. Printed in the United States of America. Developed by Nancy Hall, Inc.

CHILDREN'S PRESS and associated logos are trademarks and or registered trademarks of Scholastic Library Publishing. SCHOLASTIC and associated logos are trademarks and or registered trademarks of Scholastic Inc.

1 2 3 4 5 6 7 8 9 10 R 12 11 10 09 08 07 06 05 04 03

A NOTE TO PARENTS AND TEACHERS

Welcome to the world of the Beasties, where learning is FUN. In each of the charming stories in this series, the Beasties deal with character issues that every child can identify with. Each story reinforces appropriate concept skills for kindergartners and first graders, while simultaneously encouraging problem-solving skills. Following are just a few of the ways in which you can help children get the most from this delightful series.

Stories to be read and enjoyed

Encourage children to read the stories aloud. The rhyming verses make them fun to read. Then ask them to think about alternate solutions to some of the problems that the Beasties have faced or to imagine alternative endings. Invite children to think about what they would have done if they were in the story and to recall similar things that have happened to them.

Activities reinforce the learning experience

The activities at the end of the books offer a way for children to put their new skills to work. They complement the story and are designed to help children develop specific skills and build confidence. Use these activities to reinforce skills. But don't stop there. Encourage children to find ways to build on these skills during the course of the day.

Learning opportunities are everywhere

Use this book as a starting point for talking about how we use reading skills or math or social studies concepts in everyday life. When we search for a phone number in the telephone book and scan names in alphabetical order or check a list, we are using reading skills. When we keep score at a baseball game or divide a class into even-numbered teams, we are using math.

The more you can help children see that the skills they are learning in school really do have a place in everyday life, the more they will think of learning as something that is part of their lives, not as a chore to be borne. Plus you will be sending the important message that learning is fun.

Madeline Boskey Olsen, Ph.D.
Developmental Psychologist

Bee-Bop

Puddles

Slider

Wilbur

Pip &Zip

Flippet
Pooky
Mr. Rigby
Smudge
We're the Beasties
Toggles

What a lovely sunny day!
Flippet swims beneath a tree.
There is something in the mud.
She wonders, "What is that I see?"

Flippet rushes over to it.
"What is this? What have I found?
It looks like a treasure map!
Who has left it on the ground?"

"I must find my friends to show them!
They will want to see this, too!
Should I try to find the treasure?
Someone must know what to do!"

3 1833 04624 9592

She finds Slider in his yard.
"Slider! Come and look at this!
Might this be a treasure map?"
Slider gives a nod and hiss.

"This map leads to buried treasure!
We must go get Zip and Pip.

They are very good with numbers.
They can help us on our trip!"

"Now we are outside the schoolhouse.
On the map we start right here.

First we must pass four blue houses.
Then turn left. We must be near!"

"Mr. Rigby, come and join us!
Toggles, come and join us, too!
We will find some buried treasure!
Bee-Bop, tell us what to do!"

"First we must pass six red flowers.
Now we turn left at the store.

We must pass four rocks and turn right.
I see the house with the red door!"

"Oh, we must be very close now!
Stop before that big oak tree.

Take a left, now take a right.
Look at that! What could it be?"

"Look at all those Beastie berries!
Maybe we should stop to eat!

Have you ever seen such berries?
I would bet that these are sweet!"

"Hi there, friends! I see the map worked!
I see you knew what to do!

You thought it was buried treasure?
I guess these are treasures, too!"

"Pooky! Yes, you really tricked us!
Berry treasures! You are right!
First we can have some to eat.
Then we can have a berry fight."

TREASURE COUNT

1. How many green stripes does Slider have?

2. How many purple stripes does Slider have?

3. How many orange stripes does Slider have?

4. How many stripes does Slider have in all?

SOUNDS LIKE...

The word "flap"
sounds a lot like "map".
Can you think of other words
that sound like "map"?

LET'S TALK ABOUT IT

Flippet and Slider did not keep the treasure map a secret from the other Beasties.

1. Why do you think they wanted to tell their friends about the map?

2. Why might they have kept it a secret?

3. Pooky had a very clever way of surprising her friends. Have you ever surprised someone else by doing something that was really nice?

WORD LIST

a
all
and
are
at
be
Beastie
Bee-Bop
before
beneath
berries
berry
bet
big
blue
buried
can
close
come
could
day
do
door
eat
ever
fight
find
finds
first
Flippet
flowers
found
four
friends
get
gives
go
good
ground
guess
has
have
help
here
hi
his
hiss
house
houses
I
in
is
it
join
knew
know
leads
left
like
look
looks
lovely
map
maybe
might
Mr. Rigby
mud
must
my
near
nod
now
numbers
oak
oh
on
our
outside
over
pass
Pip
Pooky
really
red
right
rocks
rushes
schoolhouse
see
seen
she
should
show
six
Slider
some
someone
something
start
stop
store
such
summer
sweet
swims
take
tell
that
the
them
then
there
these
they
this
those
thought
to
Toggles
too
treasure
treasures
tree
tricked
trip
try
turn
us
very
want
was
we
what
who
will
with
wonders
worked
would
yard
yes
you
Zip